THE SERIAL KILLER
SERVED POUND CAKE & OTHER
SUFFICIENTLY SLANTED TALES

ALSO BY THIS AUTHOR:

By a Different Ocean

THE SERIAL KILLER
SERVED POUND CAKE & OTHER
SUFFICIENTLY SLANTED TALES

Katy E. Whittingham

First Edition: September 1st, 2015

All Rights Reserved.
Printed in the United States of America.

©2015, Stories: Katy E. Whittingham
©2015, Cover Art: Katherine L. Ehle

Principal Editor: Diane Smith
Associate Editor: Timothy Stobierski

ISBN: 978-0-9835530-9-0

Library of Congress Control Number: 2015947370

American Literature:

1   21st Century
2   Prose Fiction
3   Literary Collection
4   Individual Author, 2001 – Katy E. Whittingham

GREY SPARROW | *St. Paul, Minnesota*

For the Various Lunatics:
Maple, Oak, Violet, and Maggie

GREY SPARROW | *St. Paul, Minnesota*

CONTENTS

The Request

Peter was smoking behind the bushes to the side of St. John's, the small church he had attended since childhood. He positioned himself so he could see who came and went: his son's baseball coach, his old high school flame, currently sleeping with the married baseball coach, his work nemesis from the tannery, and so on, but no one could see him. The waiting and watching had become a weekly ritual, as Peter never felt free to walk right in as the others did.

Although he committed fewer sins than he used to, it was no easier to confess them. This paradox was what he was contemplating as he tossed his cigarette butt into the bush before wondering whether it was really a paradox at all or irony or just something that made no damn sense. Hi ex, the teacher, was the one who knew all these rules; he barely made it out of high school. As he entered, he whispered a short prayer, nothing fancy, something he picked up in AA, hoping this small effort would save him, at least until next week.

As he approached the confessional, Peter heard weeping. In his time outside on this particular day, he hadn't seen anyone enter. Curious, despite better judgment, he continued forward. The last thing he wanted to do was interrupt another poor soul's quest for forgiveness, but something felt very wrong. The curtain to the right of the confessional was quivering; he could feel a slight breeze blowing from inside.

Upon reaching to draw back the curtain, a chill and the strong smell of incense overtook him bringing him back to a different time. He held onto the curtain tightly like he was trying to squeeze something out of it. It felt like the thick maroon tablecloths his parents used at the Italian restaurant they owned when he was a kid.

Suddenly, the cry from inside turned to a plea, "God, please help me." Peter immediately recognized the voice as one that had haunted him since adolescence. He jumped back and let the curtain slip.

According to the arrangement, Father James wasn't supposed to be conducting confession on Fridays. Peter and the others hadn't asked for much, hadn't made the fuss they could have. Couldn't the church at least respect their one minor request? He momentarily forgot the cry and considered marching over to the parish office to wage a formal complaint. Before he could do this, the voice called out again, "Is someone there? I can't breathe...I think...I think I'm having a heart attack."

Peter knew he should do something. He was no saint, but he wasn't vicious. After all, hadn't he been taught forgiveness led to salvation? Wasn't it his quest to be better – to rise above what had happened to him? The elderly priest was not the same man he encountered years ago, and his death would not change anything.

Despite this sound reasoning, Peter couldn't be moved to get help because he was just the Peter he was, not the better one, not the one who could rise above what happened. He looked up at the sunlit stained glass window above. The scene depicted a young St. John the Baptist bartering before he would become the reforming zealot obsessed with the justice of God, before his head was presented on a platter. The Peter he was acknowledged nothing in this image, put his hands in his pockets, and quietly walked away.

The Lady with the Dead Dog

And it may be that in this continuity, this utter indifference to the life and death of each of us lies hidden the pledge of our eternal salvation, of the continuous movement of life on earth, of the continuous movement toward perfection.

—Anton Chekhov 1899

There was nothing dramatic about the way the woman scooped up the small tangled mound of brown and black fur from the pavement of his driveway. Adam had prepared for an emotionally intense scene. He sent his seven-year-old son, Eric, directly into the house without making him shake out his cleats, despite whiny protests and hard to answer questions. He quietly assured him that, "yes, the little dog is really dead" and "yes, kind of like the way Grandma Alma is dead but different too."

Adam then relayed the basic facts of what had happened to the dog's owner, his new neighbor, because he felt he owed her an explanation, but he was sure she saw most of it for herself from her front lawn only a few feet away.

Even if she had not seen it all for herself, just looking at the aftermath made it pretty obvious; the woman's terrier had somehow found itself in Adam's driveway and, without seeing the dog, he had run over it with his Volkswagen. Adam had not been going very fast, and it was a little car after all, but it was also a little dog. If it had been a retriever or even a hound, maybe it would have had a chance. "A good size beagle might have just needed some patching up," Adam thought without feeling.

Adam had not had the chance to meet this young lady, previous to killing her dog. She had only moved in a few days before, so he first addressed her as "Miss" because she looked to be no older than a sorority girl at the local state college. When he caught a glimpse of the large, emerald-cut diamond on her ring finger, he realized he might have made the wrong assumption. Two thin gold bands surrounded the diamond. Her pale, creaseless hands looked even younger than her face. "Poor girl; married too young," he thought, but when he looked more closely at her face as she squinted down at the remains of her dog, he saw what he might have mistaken for youth was really a simple kind of beauty that he had always admired but had become unaccustomed to.

Adam prided himself most on his ability to connect with people, even in tough situations, so he would have normally reached out and patted the woman's back. He would have found something very appropriate and consoling to say, something sincere, although in actuality entirely manufactured. There was an aura about this woman, however, that prevented the perfect execution of his normal protocol. She was so assured in her movements. Adam had noticed that in coming from her yard to his driveway, she had moved at a quick pace, appropriate for the situation, yet also seemed to glide over as if in one of the neighbor-kid's giant bubbles. Very much like Glinda the Good Witch, he thought.

Continuing with his usual movie character associations, the woman with the dead dog reminded Adam of Winona Ryder; not the real actress and not *Girl Interrupted* Winona, but more like the character she played in *Edward Scissorhands*, whatever her name was. She was petite like that and her dark hair was styled in the same kind of way. He felt a fondness toward the woman despite his newfound nervousness, and although he could not pinpoint the real reason then, it may not have been so much that she reminded him of a film character, but something he saw in her when he allowed himself to quickly glance into her dark, round eyes. Someone more perceptive might have characterized it as innocence, innocence usually reserved only for children like Eric. The comparison between the woman and his son might have meant something more profound to this more perceptive person, but Adam just felt warm and a little dizzy.

"I'm sorry. I just didn't see it," Adam finally managed to continue.

"Tuttle," the woman said. "His name was Tuttle." If her tone had been sharper, Adam might have thought she meant to achieve something by telling him this personal information. After working in client relations at an advertising agency for almost twenty years, he would have been able to pick up on her attempt to make him feel guilty. He would have been able to pick up any range of anger; the most passive sort was his specialty. Strangely, he could not detect a hint of bitterness or even sadness in the woman's voice. Thus, Adam had extreme difficulty navigating through this interaction with another person where no immediate motives could be detected.

The woman pulled out a pack of American Spirits from a pocket in her gardening apron. She put one cigarette in her mouth like she was going to smoke it, but instead she held it tight between her lips and crossed her arms over her chest. She continued on like this, all the while looking at her dog. Adam didn't have a light, so he was not able to offer her one, and she didn't offer him a cigarette.

After what felt to him like another extended silence, although merely moments, Adam forced himself to regain a hold on the situation. He offered to take care of the dog's remains, knowing this would be a delicate and nearly impossible task to perform in front of its owner if she decided to stay. There was no nice way to peal a dead dog off your driveway, and what would she want him to do with it when he did?

He had a weak stomach when it came to blood. He had once thought that he would have been an excellent doctor with his people skills and attention to detail, better in those regards than all of Eric's doctors combined. But Adam was just kidding himself when taking into consideration the actual physical work a doctor must do. He could not even watch his wife, Pam, give Eric an insulin shot. Even when she tried to force him to learn "in case of an emergency," he had refused. Now, even Eric knew how to administer the shot himself, if he needed to.

Adam thought about Eric for the first time, consciously at least, since he sent him into the house. He pictured him crying over this woman's dog: Turtle, Tobey, whatever the dog's name is or was. So odd, Adam thought. He found it difficult to accept that Eric was the type of boy who was brave enough to give himself a shot if he had to, but emotionally ill-equipped to deal with the death of a dog he never knew. This was just another confirmation he was his mother's child.

Of course, Pam, Adam's wife, would not have approved of Eric being in the house for so long by himself. "What were you thinking?" she would ask him as she often did, never really wanting an answer from him. This would only be the case if she found out Eric had been left, and in the midst of a fit over the dead dog. Eric might just tell her.

The woman thanking him for his kind offer roused Adam from his thoughts. To Adam's relief, she told him she would take care of the remains herself. The woman excused herself and crossed into her yard and into a large aluminum shed. Again her movements were a mixture of purpose, grace, and magic. The shed she retreated into had just been put up the day before by a man who Adam now knew must be the woman's husband.

"The husband," Adam thought in sudden realization. How was the man who put up the shed going to react to the death of his wife's dog? Maybe he would come over and confront him, fight him, sue him. He didn't know this man, and just because the woman appeared to hold no grudge, the husband could be another story.

Adam had never even seen the woman's husband, but Pam had. She saw him from their kitchen window putting together that very shed. The man had sprawled pre-cut pieces and parts of what looked like a complete do-it-yourself kit and was walking around with an open instruction booklet, examining each piece and arranging them into a series of piles. "He's very muscular," Pam told Adam, "maybe even into weight lifting; he's that big." Adam was not jealous of these comments because he knew that didn't match his wife's type, or at least what he perceived his wife's type to be. "You should have seen how quickly he put that thing up," she commented.

Adam promptly told his wife that in his experience "things of quality are not meant to be put up quickly." He didn't like that his neighbor had put up such a trashy looking shed. "It doesn't match the decorum of the neighborhood," he told her. In all honestly, he was amazed that Pam, his own wife and a woman who came from money, was either unable or unwilling to make the distinction between a shed that could be sitting for sale in front of the enormous Save-and-Shop out on Route 30 and the type of solid, well-crafted structures that were expected in their part of town. He went on to provide a list of reasons why the shed was a poor choice, but Pam was no longer really listening to him. She had the radio on trying to catch the weather and was cutting yellow peppers for the quesadillas she was making for supper.

"I don't see what the big deal is," Pam said when there was a momentary lapse in Adam's listing. "Don't people have the right to put up anything they want in their own yard? It's not like we live in a gated community."

Adam was very excited with himself that he had saved the best part for last. Pam was always acting smarter than him, more laid back, more reasonable, but he had correctly anticipated her response to his criticism of the shed, and she had fallen into his trap. "That's just it," he said trying for a matter of fact tone, yet sounding smug instead. "The shed is ¼ of a foot on Dickerson's property. I consulted the original contractor's map that I ordered last year. I consulted it twice!"

This information did not have the effect he desired, and without missing a beat, Pam asked him if he had actually gone over, "trespassing no less," to measure the amount their new neighbors' shed was over their other neighbor's property line. "If you did, I feel very embarrassed for you," she said. "Besides," she added. "Let Dick worry if the shed is on his property."

Adam was furious and stormed into his home office. Once again Pam was asking a question that required no answer. It was irritating especially when he was trying to prove a point. It didn't matter that he was the one who was actually right. Of course, it didn't directly affect him, but he couldn't go to Dick Dickerson for help. He wouldn't care that the shed was on his property. He had bigger problems. He had the lifelong affliction of being named Dick Dickerson for starters, and Dr. Richard Dickerson's wife had left him for her Pilates' instructor only the summer before.

Now she lived in Costa Rica and didn't even have a proper address to send divorce papers to. Dick was also being sued by a woman he performed surgery on who said he left her with uneven and sensation-less breasts. This wasn't the first time either. Even if Adam were able to make Dick understand that he was being taken advantage of by the crafty, yet tacky, new neighbors, he wouldn't actually do anything about it.

As far as Adam knew, the only thing he did, when he wasn't in court or in bed weeping, was drink sour apple martinis and watch his absent wife's complete collection of *Friends* episodes on DVD. Dick's wife had been told sometime in the late 90s that she looked like the character of Rachel and had become mildly obsessed with the idea. To be fair, she did bare a slight resemblance, if perfect television Rachel gained twenty pounds, spent twenty years in the sun, and had twenty nips and tucks under her belt.

Instead of wasting his time with Dick, Adam planned to talk directly to the new neighbors about the unfortunate situation with the shed, out of courtesy for all parties involved. He would bring over a Freihofer's coffeecake and divert casual, neighborly banter into serious talk about the shed. If they were decent people they would take it down immediately and honor Dick's property rights. In his current state, they wouldn't likely have a chance to talk with Dick at length and wouldn't need to know that he didn't care or even know his rights were being violated. Maybe the husband wouldn't bother putting the shed up again at all, or maybe, under Adam's suggestion, he would move it to the backyard facing a wooded area, so at least passing cars would not see it.

Adam had delayed this planned interaction with the new neighbors because he had a strong suspicion that they were not decent people after all or why would they have put up the shed in the first place? Just because something made sense to him, didn't mean that these classless newcomers would follow his line of thinking.

Pam had, more often in recent years, chastised Adam for his lack of tact. However, while waiting in his own driveway, standing over the neighbor's dead dog and not doing anything to help the woman knocking around in the same shed he had been brooding about, even Adam was aware enough to know that it was, not only presently a very poor to time to bring up the ¼ foot, but there would likely never be a good time in the foreseeable future. He began to feel so uncomfortable that he thought he might get sick and stepped back in a motion to flee toward his house, but within seconds the woman was back, and he was stuck in his tracks.

She still had the cigarette in her mouth. A metal toolbox was dangling from her Snow White hands. Resting on top of the box was a magazine, a paint scraper, and a pair of gardening gloves freshly coated with soil. She looked up briefly as Adam changed his stance to face back to the scene with his hands on his hips, and then she went right to work. He was amazed, almost horrified, at the precision in which the woman scrapped the dog's body off the driveway, propped it onto a copy of *Glamour*, and slid it into the empty toolbox. When she latched the lid, she put the box on the ground, took off her gardening gloves, and offered Adam her hand. "Sarah," she said.

Adam looked at the porcelain hand, then at the closed box on the ground, then at that exquisite hand again, then at the cigarette, and then at the perfectly folded gardening gloves resting on top of the box. Had he even seen her put them there? He finally reached out his hand in front of him, but she had to move in closer to shake it. Her hand was warm from being inside of the glove. "Adam Hart," he said with great effort under his breath and barely audible.

"Ah, Adam," she said. Then, "Adam, you have a son?" It was as if she was asking and telling him at the same time. Coming back to his senses, Adam wondered if it was all women who insisted on asking questions they seemed to already know the answer to. He nodded and reluctantly let go her hand.

∞

Three days after the incident, Adam found himself peering into the new neighbors' sitting room window from his yard, trying to appear inconspicuous, while adjusting his sprinkler system. They had not yet put up blinds or curtains, which he found a little odd, but he was happy to find there was little to obstruct his view. The woman was not currently in the sitting room, but it looked like she had been. He could see a coffee mug, although he imagined she drank only tea, on the table and a book, spine up and spread. The television was on and a local public access correspondent appeared on the screen, but he assumed that she probably had the volume off, while she was reading. Adam's own mother, when she was alive, used to keep the television on, but turned down, just to give herself "a little company" after he and his older brother left to start lives of their own. The woman, this Sarah, seemed to be alone a great deal of the time too.

Adam still had not even seen her husband. He saw his truck there late in the evenings, but it would be gone again by early morning. He was no longer afraid of the husband's reaction to the death of the dog, as he had received no calls and no visits. This freedom allowed him think more about Sarah out of the context of her dead dog, and he had been thinking about her pretty continually.

Although he had strained to see the print and images on the book's cover, he couldn't make out any details without his distance glasses. If he just knew the title, he could pick up a copy at the bookstore he passed on his way to work, read it, and then manipulate a conversation in which he recommended the book to her. She would be shocked and tell him she was reading the same book. Wouldn't that be something?

Pam had been after Adam to adjust their sprinkler's spray for weeks, but was particularly adamant when she "re-reminded" him, her word, about it that morning. "It doesn't cover the entire lawn and shoots across the sidewalk," she complained. "People have to walk into the road to avoid it." He had first thought to be humorous by responding that it was less expensive than a security system, but he didn't share this response because lately his kind humor was not humor that Pam seemed to appreciate.

"Just wait until Mr. Ferriera hobbles by with his cane and slips on the wet pavement," she continued. "Then we will have a lawsuit, like Dick's, on our hands to add to all of our problems." When she said "our problems," Adam understood what she really meant was an all-encompassing collection of issues that were caused by him and dealt with by her. "People will say," she went on, " 'He sure doesn't brake for small animals, so I guess further crippling the old and feeble is not much of a stretch.' " She laughed after she said this, whole-heartedly and without discretion, before going back to something other than talking to him. He was surprised that she could be so flippant about the dog considering how upset she was over its death, but it seemed it was now okay, for her at least, to make light of it. It was not surprising to him, however, how apparent it had become that Pam didn't care whether Adam still appreciated *her* kind of humor.

∞

The woman continued to be on Adam's mind during the days that followed, but he hadn't again had the opportunity to speak with her. He had so many questions and only his own imagined answers. Over time, he had decided that the woman with the dead dog looked more like Mia Farrow than Winona Ryder, but, of course, a younger version of Farrow and with darker hair. Sarah wasn't beautiful by catalog standards. Those kinds of women Adam saw every day in the ad biz, but her features struck him, caught him off guard, moved him in a way he was not entirely comfortable with.

He had asked himself whether he wanted to have sex with this woman, and he honestly didn't know. It bothered him that he began now to think consciously of Eric when he thought of her and what his real intentions were. Again, instead of trying to understand this connection, he started to resent the distraction.

One particularly troublesome memory continued to play back for him. It was the last time Adam took Eric to the park before school started back. Eric had wanted to be pushed on the swings. Adam told him he was too old to be pushed; he was going to be in second grade, and that he should learn, as boys half his age already had, to pump his legs, to get himself going. Adam had tried to teach him this many times before, but Eric would just sit limp on the swing, slowly swaying his legs in circular motion, not even really trying. As he always did, Adam told Eric he would provide a few pushes to get him started. As he pushed he yelled, "Now, pump, pump!"

Not only did Eric not pump his legs as directed, but once again, as soon as he reached some real height, he dragged his feet in the dirt to slow himself down. On this particular day, Adam was unwilling to put up with the familiar routine. He jerked the chains of the swing to bring Eric to a complete stop. He told him they were leaving that instant, and that there would be no monkey bars and no Burger Hut afterward. Even without the stares from some young, hippy parents by the Mary-go-round, Adam knew he was overreacting, but Eric, head down, was already following him to the car, so it was too late to modify his behavior.

As his lousy luck would have it, when Adam drove them home, they got stuck at the traffic light right in front of Burger Hut. It was a long light, and Adam wasn't very angry anymore. It appeared that someone had had a birthday party, and the kids, younger than Eric, were filing out with goodie bags and balloons. An overweight girl with freckled skin let go of a purple balloon and watched it sail up over the Price Mart building. It was sunny, and Adam couldn't tell if the girl was crying or delighted. If Eric had asked, Adam would have stopped as they had planned, but he didn't, and when the light changed, he drove them home.

Eric didn't even tell Pam what happened when they got back as Adam had expected he would. She asked how the park was, and they both said fine.

She probably was suspicious, but she didn't push the issue. Adam had to give her credit in that regard; she usually didn't try to interfere in his relationship with Eric despite her growing resentment. She was a good mother and did what was best for their son.

This may have been why Adam had never seriously considered cheating on Pam before. He had his fair share of opportunity, and in his usual list format he could have weighed the pros and cons, mainly the pros and cons for himself, of course. But, it just wasn't something he thought about taking action on.

At times, he didn't really want Pam anymore, but he also didn't really want anyone else either. There were times when he could see why a woman would be desirable, but there were times when Pam seemed okay too. His wife may have been frustrated by him and condescending to him, but others didn't catch on. Men they knew envied him for marrying a woman like Pam with beauty, intelligence, and charm. After eleven years of marriage, he may no longer have appreciated these qualities, but having others appreciate her in this way had been enough.

He hadn't seen anything wrong with this justification. At least, he was still there, and, in his experience, it was completely natural for people to fall out of love. Like when his father left his mother with two young children to go off with his much younger Pamela or Mrs. Dickerson, leaving poor, pathetic Dick with nothing but some DVDS to remember her by. Love was an unexplainable thing and not something that was meant to last.

Unlike his own father or Dick's wife, Adam would not allow himself to be bullied by this inevitability. No matter how he felt or what happened, if anything, between him and the neighbor woman, Adam would not leave Pam. There was Eric to consider, and he didn't know what he would do if he couldn't see him on a day-to-day basis.

Eric had been diagnosed with diabetes when he was only three years old, and Pam had, and continued to, handle the situation much better than Adam. Eric was sensitive, yet, physically, an incredibly resilient child. His mother was also responsible for both of these qualities. Eric was never going to be the sports' star that Adam had dreamed of, and because of their differences, no one would call him "his father's son," but something slowly began to take the place of his old expectations for him, and Adam needed that boy more every day.

∞

Two weeks after the dog's demise, Pam was preparing to take Eric for a long weekend at her mother's in Albany. "So whatever happened with the lady and the dead dog thing?" she asked as she prepared a snack bag of carrots and celery for Eric to take on their road trip.

"What do you mean?" Adam asked, trying to sound coy. He purposely didn't look up from his paper, so she would not see his eyes.

"Well, you killed a family pet. I just wondered if there were any consequences that followed for you, or if you just went on with your life as usual, unbothered and unaffected," she said. She seemed to be trying for sarcasm, but just sounded sad.

"It's not a family: just a woman and a man, and he is gone half the time, and I didn't mean to do it. It's not like it was a crime, and don't forget the dog was on my, *our* property," he said.

"Oh, I forgot about your preoccupation with property," she snapped. And when he didn't respond she added as an afterthought, "And, you know, or maybe you don't because you don't think of things like this, but maybe that dog was everything to this woman. Maybe because she has no children and her husband is working all of the time. Maybe the dog was her only...thing."

Adam shrugged, and Pam shook her head disapprovingly. "Did you even get her name? I want to go see her when I get back. I should have gone over before, but frankly I was embarrassed."

"No!" Adam shouted.

"What?" Pam said and turned around to face him. She looked straight into him forcing him to at last lift to meet her glare.

"I mean, no, I didn't get her name," he said trying to recover.

"Of course, you didn't," she said as she snatched the plastic baggie from the counter and went about preparing to leave.

∞

An hour and a half after his wife and son's departure, Adam was busy trying to hide an empty bottle of Merlot under a week's worth of newspapers in the recycling bin on the back porch. The wine was a gift from Pam's sister Leslie after her annual spring trip to France. It was old and expensive, but the only alcohol in the house. Neither Pam nor Adam were big drinkers. Pam had an occasional glass of bubbly on special occasions or when amongst her blueblood family of lushes, but that was about it. The missing wine might have gone unnoticed, but Leslie would be in the city the next week for a business meeting. If she stopped by on her way out, Pam would get the gifted wine out for the grape fiend to slurp up.

As Adam had been drinking, he had also been thinking. It was Friday. On Fridays, Adam had noted, the husband's truck came home even later than usual. Maybe Friday was a big day in whatever business he was in. Maybe he was having an affair on her. No matter really, he thought as he began to come around to the idea that regardless, maybe it was now a good time for him to go check in on her. This idea became more and more appealing and doable as he drank. He felt really confident and quite well overall. He made a mental note that he should drink more often.

Before very long, Adam found himself on the front porch of the woman's house. He stared at the brass doorbell. It was cold outside, but he felt flushed, in a good way. "The bell or nothing," he thought as he finally lifted his heavy hand up to the fixture and watched as his waving index finger pressed the tiny circle in the middle. For such a little action, it produced the loudest and longest lasting ringing sound imaginable. Having been shocked by this intense sound, when the woman swung open the door, Adam didn't expect it.

"Sarah," he said trying to cover up that he was stumbling backwards the way a drunken person does when their body starts to betray their best intentions of appearing sober.

She was wearing a gray silk pantsuit. Her hair, although short, was pulled back from her forehead with a headband. This look made her look older. Not old, just older.

"Adam, come on in," she said almost as if she was expecting him. Since she apparently was not surprised in the least by his visit, he wasn't going to make up excuses when there wasn't a need for any. He felt his drunkenness more now that he was in the presence of another person, and he had to be careful not to talk too much.

"I hope I'm not disturbing you at dinner time. Is your husband at home?" he asked. The woman told him that he was not disturbing her, and also, what he already knew, that her husband was not at home. She told him that she was having a glass of sherry, and asked if he would like some. Despite his newly acquired appreciation for alcohol, he maintained the slightest bit of good judgment and said no thank you.

They sat down on the couch. It was a loveseat really, so they were closer than strangers would be in most situations, but there were no other seats to be had, which she apologized for and told him some of their larger belongings had been delayed in the move. Her breath smelled very sweet. Adam didn't know if sherry was some kind of brandy or a port, whatever that was. He had only seen it on desert menus when they were out to eat at fancy places with his in-laws.

Despite the lack of furnishings, the wall space was almost completely covered with black and white photographs. The pictures were mostly of a man who Adam concluded must be the husband. He was more handsome than Adam had anticipated, but black and white always made people look better than they did in real life. Judging by the photographs the husband looked to be a sportsman of sorts and also some other choice roles Adam quickly characterized: a jerk, a snob, a first class asshole. Adam's assessment may not have been fair, but his advertising expertise allowed him to trust his impression of the images and the face value they provided.

The woman observed Adam observing her work. "I'm a photographer," she said taking a cigarette out and putting it in her mouth unlit. "My husband thinks all the photos are overkill. He's only letting me keep them up until he has time to repaint the walls," she murmured with the cigarette still clasped between her lips.

"I like them," Adam managed but could see why a room full of pictures, especially almost all of him, might be creepy. It could have been the wine, but they seemed alive. There were just so many of them, all staring, all expecting.

"Do you need a light?" Adam asked pointing to the cigarette, while immediately remembering he had no light to provide.

She seemed absorbed in the photographs herself and his question came off as an interruption. "Oh, no. Trying to quit," she said without further explanation.

Adam's own focus turned to one photograph of the husband with a captain's hat on steering a boat with his elbow. His other arm was raised in salutatory greeting. What an absolute tool, Adam thought enjoying the mounting criticism he was building against the man until he noticed a detail he missed at first glance.

There was a small creature on the man's lap with its fur blown wildly back by the wind to reveal two eyes the color, size, and shape of lumps of coal. Could it be the little dead dog? A disturbing pattern started to emerge as Adam began to frantically scan all of the photographs on the wall. The little urchin was everywhere: in a tropical scene under a palm tree, in front of a Christmas tree, in a shopping cart, in the husband's truck bed, in a bike basket, on a sleigh in the snow, next to a fish hanging from a line, at a barbecue, with a bone, by a fire, at the beach, with a stick, at the park, on a picnic.

"Your dog," Adam managed, feeling compelled by its presence and possibly a small amount of guilt brought about more from the wine than any real reflection. "You must miss him."

"He was Charlie's dog. I actually hated the rat, resented the shit out of him," she said. "Charlie doesn't want to try for more children. He thought bringing Tuttle home would appease my motherly needs; it didn't."

Adam's confusion must have shown on his face because the woman quickly continued. "I had three miscarriages, then the last one was stillborn at eight months."

"Oh, I'm sorry," Adam said.

The woman didn't seem to hear him or just took for granted that is what any normal person would say in response.

"You know, you, Adam…" she said pointing her cigarette at him in an almost accusatory way. "You are very lucky to have a son. You are lucky to have a family and have purpose. My husband is gone all of the time as you might have noticed. We have drifted apart over our losses and are not the same people; maybe not even people that should be together anymore." Silence.

Then as if continuing a monologue in a play, Sarah rose and continued, "Get this, he only married me because I was pregnant, the first time. An accident. Who knew we would end up here? I used to have a passion for all kinds of things, including my work. Now it's hard to even have a reason to get out of bed in the morning. I'm thirty-five, and my life might as well be over… But, shit, God damn it, listen to me," she apologized as she sat back down. "I'm so embarrassed to put this on you! You just asked about the dog. Yes, Charlie misses the dog very much, bordering on way too much, to be honest. I guess I have had too much time by myself lately, too much time to think, and I have forgotten how to properly talk to other people. I'm so sorry."

There was finally more silence and Adam shifted on the cushion closer to the armrest and away from her. He held in his breath like he did when he was young and heard his parents fighting. This woman who was such a mystery only moments before had managed to reveal a life story in a short collection of sentences. A sad story; one Adam hadn't anticipated and didn't know if he wanted to be a part of. He thought he might throw up or explode. Her audience was ready to leave.

"You shouldn't feel that way," Adam said as he let out a breath.

"Why not?"

He waited thinking this was one of those women kind of questions that didn't need a response, but the woman continued to have an expectant look on her face.

"Umm, I guess I meant children aren't everything. It's seems like you travel a lot by the pictures. Do a lot of activities. You can't do that as much when you have kids. We, my wife and I, we don't do anything much anymore, not by ourselves anyway, and my son, he has a lot of problems. Health issues. He has diabetes. His mother babies him a lot. He's really different, or I mean, we, my son and I, Eric and I, aren't anything alike."

"But you love him?" she asked.

"Well, of course, I love him," Adam said. He was now really, really wishing not to be at the woman's house at all. He felt sorry for her and all of her problems, but he had no words that could help her or even support his previous reasoning. He felt strange to have a son, something she wanted so desperately and tried so hard for, and he had done nothing in his life to deserve Eric. Being a father was just something that happened to him.

"Wait here just a minute," the woman said and walked into the other room and out of sight. Adam wondered how he could make a clean break. He fumbled in his pocket for his cell phone to make it sound like he was getting a call, but he had left it at the house.

When she returned she sat even closer to Adam. She leaned in, and he thought she was going to kiss him. He could smell the sweetness again. He tipped his head back on his neck and closed his eyes.

He decided that he wouldn't initiate anything, but he wouldn't fight her advances either. He was nothing now, but exhausted, and he had come this far for better or worse.

With his eyes still closed, he felt a warm, wet, almost coarse thing pry open his lips. It took a moment for him to process the strange sensation before he opened his eyes. Sarah, the focus of his fantasies for the past few weeks, was vigorously scrubbing the inside of his mouth with a damp dishrag. There was nothing less fantastic and more real than a dishrag.

Adam pushed away the cloth, got up with stiff legs, and went for the door. "You just had some purplish stains on your teeth," she said. "I was trying to clean you up, so I could take your picture. That's what I do. I take pictures."

"Your shed," Adam murmured and continued to flee. "What?" the woman asked after him. Then, "wait." She sounded desperate like she needed something from him, but Adam had managed to get the door open and was halfway to his garage and safety.

The light was on in the front room of his home. He was almost sure he had shut all of the lights off before he made the ill-fated decision to get to know the lady next door. He couldn't get the garage door open, but hadn't remembered locking the front one, so he started across the yard.

As he approached the stone steps, he saw Pam standing in the door. The porch light illuminated her and little bugs swarmed all around. She looked like an apparition until she spoke.

"We saw you next door. Through their window. Eric and I both saw you. You looked like you were kissing the lady with the dead dog. Adam, were you kissing her?" she asked.

"No, I wasn't. I swear. Why are you home? Is Eric okay? Did he have an episode?"

Pam crossed her arms. "The thruway is closed. There was an accident, a fatal accident. We decided to come back for the night and leave in the morning. Why were you kissing that woman, Adam?" she asked again as if he had not yet responded to her question. Although she wanted to appear calm, she seemed hurt and scared. She seemed confused and shaken, and Adam felt more love for her then than he had in a very long time.

"I didn't kiss her! I went to talk about the shed. She's a photographer. I had stains on my teeth from drinking wine," he started to ramble.

"Drinking? Adam, you know what, on second thought, don't even try to explain," Pam returned. "You have really outdone yourself here. I have come to expect some downright shitty behavior from you, but I never expected this. I'm going to try to put Eric to bed; he's very upset right now. Just leave us alone, please."

Adam began again, but she put her hand up and turned her back on him. He watched as the screen door snapped her in and she took a waiting Eric's hand and began to ascend the stairs. As the outsider, he could see this was an image too. Beautiful, more beautiful, and sad, sadder than anything he had ever seen.

He wanted to call after his little family. He wanted to tell them that no matter how bad the scene looked, it wasn't his fault that the woman tricked him, that she had problems like everyone else, that he wasn't thinking clearly before, but now… Now.

Instead he sat on the steps, feeling very sorry, mostly for himself. "And," he said finally looking down at the ground with no one left to argue with, "it wasn't even her dog."

The Serial Killer Served Pound Cake

"You don't have to speak, Mama. I know it's difficult. Try and rest," daughter says as she pats mother's matted hair.

"I have some things I should tell you," mother responds, trying to prop herself up on the pillows behind her. "Things I done, things that I have some regret about now. Now, that I'm looking back on it all." Mother leans forward slightly with purpose, while daughter stares at an exposed pillowcase shadowed with sick sweat.

"Whatever it is, let it go. What good could come from dredging it up? Let the past be and put yourself in God's hands," daughter reassures as she gently pushes mother back from her boosted position. "Rest, Mama, dear."

"I only wanted to be a good mother to you."

"You are a good mother, Mama. Always have been, and nothing you could tell me now would change that."

Mother moves the rosary beads in her hands like she is working a pulley and coughs to clear the fluids of death from her throat. Daughter walks to the edge of the room to a metal table on wheels and pours water from a mustard yellow plastic pitcher into a cup with a bendable straw. She quickly adds the thickening powder, so that mother doesn't see her do it. She returns to mother and carefully positions the straw between her coated white lips. Mother takes a sip, and the water gurgles as it struggles to go down.

"Please, just hear me out," mother pleads. "I know I have told you this many times, but even though you're adopted, when I first laid eyes on you, I knew you was more my daughter than if I had you myself." Daughter nods as she has heard this part many times. "And," mother continues. "No one was going to take you away from me or hurt you in anyway. It was my duty in this life to make sure of it."

Mother stops to cough up some of the water that she just drank mixed with a little blood, and daughter gingerly wipes her mouth with a dark towel, a towel she brought to the hospital herself to save mother from seeing the red spots that are more and more frequent. Daughter had once worked as an aide in the very hospital where she now stood over her dying mother and never could understand why hospitals seemed to contain so much white: the towels, the sheets, the walls. All so vulnerable to stain.

"All good mothers protect their children, Mama, and I appreciate everything you done for me."

"As you know your birth parents are dead, but there's a little more to the story. They was heroin addicts as you also know and for good reason couldn't care for you when you was born. It was supposed to be a closed adoption with no contact. None! But when that birth mother got herself clean, she come to look for you. She said her rights had been violated, if you can believe that, because of the state she was in at the time she gave you up. She was stupid enough to stay with the father who was still using, but she thought if she got you back that somehow he would decide to quit too, and you'd be one happy family.

She got our address somehow, showed right up at the door, and told me all this like I was supposed to feel sorry for her! She had some beat up lookin' toys and books in plastic grocery bags. She wanted to give the old used things to you herself like they were these great presents. The whole thing was ridiculous; she was so selfish, so self-serving. Still, I was stricken; stricken with fear that if she got it together, was able to scrounge up enough cash to hire a lawyer, and went to court, she, being your biological mother and all, would somehow win and take you away from me because as you know by now life isn't always fair."

Mother seems like she is done with what she has to say, but before daughter can speak, she proceeds with her story, squinting as if trying to focus on an image in the distance. "I seen how she looked at you playing on the floor through the picture window after I told her to take an everlasting hike. I just couldn't let her take you, Emmie!" Mother's chest heaves as she tries to pull in breath, but she looks energized and almost crazed too like someone who just crossed the finish line after a very long race.

"Wow, I didn't know any of that happened… but it's still the past. The woman didn't take me, Mama, and everything worked out in the end. You're really going to strain yourself going on like this though…with your stories. Try and rest."

"The past; it's here now like a visitor in the room. I need to answer to it." Mother intently scans the room with anticipation as if she expects the past to call out and introduce itself.

"You don't even sound like yourself. I wish you would rest, but, of course, if it helps to talk, I'm here to listen. Just try to keep your voice down, stay calm, and try not to be so dramatic. To be honest, it's kind of creeping me out."

"See, I never gave that woman, your so called mother, a chance. Before she could try to get you back, I set their shambles of a house on fire in the middle of the night. I knew a place like that wouldn't have no smoke alarms, and it didn't. I knew the police wouldn't bother to look into the deaths of a couple of junkies, and they didn't."

"Mama, now, that just didn't happen. You are going too far. You have to stop this, it's the medicine talkin'."

"Then when were fourteen and your choir director from down the street gave Kristy Gavin the solo you was meant to sing. I invited her over for pound cake and sweet tea and put antifreeze in it. Back then they didn't have the tests and ways to figure those things out. Thank the Lord Jesus of Nazareth for that."

"Mrs. Bennett died of kidney failure, Mama. Stop, now; I'm being serious."

"Oh my, it seems to be much easier if I can get it all out, quick like, doesn't it? Okay, so next was Jillian, that hussy. Said she was your best friend then went behind your back and spread rumors about you. I wanted to skin her alive. Make her pay mighty."

The daughter with her finger on the nurses' call button had just been contemplating getting help, even though she's slightly embarrassed to bother anyone with this nonsense. From her past work, she is familiar with the craziness dying can bring about in people, but it's different with *her* mother. Always such a sensible and pious woman, it's hard to see her completely lose it, but mother's last words seemed to reduce her panic and daughter removes her finger from the button and shakes some tension from her shoulders.

"Okay, now you're really being silly. Jillian is alive and well and living in Texas. She works for a news station. You seen the article in the paper about her just as I did," daughter says with the satisfaction of thinking she has ended this ridiculous game and maybe can go back to properly seeing mother off from this world.

But mother responds with equal satisfaction and a little pride, "True, I knew someone that close may be traced back to us, so I hit her where it hurts instead. I ran that sad excuse of a boyfriend Jimmy's motorcycle off the road by Potter's Drop. Same stupid boy who had the nerve to turn you down when you asked him to the May Dance in 7th grade. The way he drove that thing; no one even questioned that one."

"Mama, I'm going to ask you one more time to stop this. Jimmy died in an accident. An accident. I'm going to get a nurse in here. I don't know what they are giving you, but I'm going to find out and put an end to these hallucinations." This time, she starts for the door.

"There's just one more," mother says more tentatively.

"One?" the daughter quietly repeats to the door before slowly turning around. She is unsure for only a moment before horror pushes its way in. Like her mother saw the past, fear is now a visitor in the room for daughter, and she slowly steps back away from it towards the cart with the water pitcher. She tries to lean on the cart, but it gives way. She quickly regains her footing and rests her sweaty back on the wall instead.

"No, Mama, don't you say anything about him. Not even a lie. I just can't handle even a damned lie right now. Do you hear me, woman?"

Mother closes her eyes, summoning strength to continue. She doesn't want to hurt daughter – that's the last thing she wants, but nothing can be left out. It all needs to be said. She shakes her head with an apologetic look on her face.

"No, no, do you hear me? I know what you are going to say, and I won't believe you, but I just can't take to hear anything negative about Daddy."

"He was set to leave us. Did you know that? He was going to go off to Florida with that bartender woman, Ellen, and was going to use up all your college funds and such."

"Mama, I said no. Don't do it, I mean it, please."

"Him, I just shot in the head. I made him write a letter of apology first. Said if it was good enough I would let him live. Maybe I would have too, but it was shit. Not a genuine bone in that tiny bastard's body. It ended up serving as his suicide note, but you know; you read it."

"God help you, Mama, if anything of this is true. For heaven's sake, you are a Christian woman."

"That's just it, darling. I wanted to do the will of God, but I was a mama first...and good motherin', it's a bitch of a job."

"Mama, I'm going to get the nurse; you're turning so red."

"No, don't you bother; it's time. I can feel the fire rising from my toes as they say. It won't be so long now, and God may not be whose I going to see, but my only regret is leaving you, my sweet Emmie.

No one will ever love you like your mother. I hope you understand that better now as I won't be here to show you no more."

And whether the daughter would admit it or not, despite it all, she was beginning to understand a great many things…much, much better now.

Our Hipster Neighbor

In the apartment downstairs, her young, freckleless hand is weighed down with the crystal lead of a green, ornate, 1970s wine glass leaving the scribbled lines of her palm exposed, so he, the one she thinks she loves with all of an unpracticed heart, can read their pretend future. Trendy wisdom may wear out like the t-shirts he wears two decades older than he, but her questions are left unanswered because they go unasked.

Being Linda Marten

I wasn't always her. I used to be me, and I had a cat named Bobby Mac and a job working for the post office, though I wasn't a carrier because of my bad knees. I fed Bobby at 6:00 and then at 5:30 when I got home from my job for the United States Postal Service.

First the phone messages started asking for Linda, and I noticed there were always two blackbirds sitting on the wire outside my window. A friend told me birds use wire for their nests sometimes and can really mess up your connection, but these birds were just sitting, always sitting. No, I said to the phone voices then. No, I said, I was not Linda Marten, until finally they convinced me.

Bobby was old, but not so old for a cat. If he were a dog he might have been long dead, but he was always old, old since he started coming around. He was a stray, and I adopted him because I loved cats. I loved that cat. Linda, they told me, was allergic.

Over the winter, my face slowly changed and the birds finally flew away. The mail began to come with her name on it, and I went into work to report the problem, but they told me that a Linda Marten did not work for them; they said I did not work for them. They didn't recognize me; I didn't recognize me.

There was a time when I didn't leave the house or talk to anyone aside from Bobby because when you don't know who you are, conversation becomes quite difficult. A simple errand like going for groceries became almost impossible and was pointless because I no longer liked my favorite foods like tuna salad with diced pickles on white crustless bread or peanut butter and jelly Ritz crackers like Mama had always made for me as an afterschool snack.

I'm not sure how long I stayed inside. It wasn't until I woke up at 6:00 to feed Bobby on the coldest day I can remember that I ventured back into the world. My punctual cat was not at the door waiting. He was missing. The only part of my heart that was still mine broke in two. I called the police, but the responding officer seemed less than concerned.

"Hey, what's the difference between a cat and a dog?" the officer asked, "dogs come when they're called; cats take a message and get back to you later."

His levity did not ease my fears, and I told him, frankly, I didn't know anything about dogs, but Bobby never missed breakfast. I told him quite definitely that Bobby did not ignore my calls. Without offering to come by and help, he suggested I check with the neighbors, but no one wanted to open their door to me. Their faces were familiar, but mine was strange and dirty. My reflection in the glass was strange and dirty.

I went home to wash my face and try to cover up my Linda mask when I noticed that I had a phone message. Excitedly, I pressed the button hoping it was news about my dear Bobby. "Linda," the message began, "you need to stop coming to look for our cat, you witch. My daughter is crying right now, afraid you will take her Putty away again. Do you like making little girls cry, Linda?"

No. No, it seemed Linda did not, and with that, the transition was complete. I gave up. What choice did I have? When you have a cat named Bobby and a job with the United States Postal Service, and then you don't, well, you might as well just accept yourself as Linda Marten.

Morning Edition

Aura's husband, Lionel, known as Rusty to his many friends, was dead. 52. Heart attack. Aside from not hearing their front door swing open and smack close when the tannery down the road let out for the day and not being awoken in the night by heavy and persistent snoring, the day to day life of his wife of thirty years changed very little.

She took off exactly one week, her earned vacation time from the bank, to take care of his arrangements: a cremation, the announcement in the local *Morning Edition*, and two hours of viewing time followed by a funeral service at the only church in town. That was pretty much all there was to it. Rusty had turned out to be as simple in death as he was in life, and Aura probably could have taken off only half of a week.

They had not been able to have children, so the money, consisting of some modest savings, retirement, and insurance, was now all hers. And Aura didn't think twice about what she would do with it.

She opened a separate account at the same bank where she worked, also the only one in town, to keep the money where it could remain safe, secure, and untouched. Her thrifty nature would not allow her to think beyond this step or entertain questions like – what would happen to it when she died?

Rusty was buried in the cemetery outside of town where his own parents had been buried twenty some years earlier. His father and mother both died in their early fifties too, but this was not so unusual in their little foothills town. Most residents were now willing to consider what they had vehemently disputed for years; the mills and tanneries could be at least partially to blame for the premature death and disease that seemed to plague them, but what would they do if the only remaining operations closed? Things were hard enough with almost all of the work already moved overseas.

Rusty worked at the same leather tannery for almost twenty-five years and was very well liked. When the news of his death got around, the wives of his coworkers dropped off full meals to Aura in tin foil covered casserole dishes, and when they later returned to pick up their cookware and asked if there was anything they could do, they seemed to honestly mean it. The food they provided was heavy and enough to feed an army. Aura hated to see things go to waste; she also wasn't much for small talk or pleasantries, but she could appreciate the women's time and sentiment.

Aura's own coworkers at the bank took a slightly more detached approach. She had a pile of about seven envelopes with her name written on them on the desk she shared when she returned to work. Upon opening the cards, she recognized the variety of sayings and picture prints from browsing the racks at the dollar store in the next town over. She didn't fault her coworkers for this and was almost more comfortable with their lack of effort than the tannery wives' good deeds. Not willing to pay more than she had to, she had purchased cards at the store too, and she knew that she never had the way with people that Rusty did. She wasn't the type of person who one would go out of their way for. She wasn't a full price card type of girl.

It may have seemed strange to some that Rusty married Aura in the first place, but how could they understand the circumstances behind their union? They had both made the big move to "the city," Albany, and come to work at the same the doll factory. They were acquainted with each other already, of course, being from the same small suburb forty miles west, but Rusty was three years older and ran with a different crowd in high school. As so many others had, he didn't pay much attention to Aura when they were in school. What might have brought them together in their new environment was that they had both dared to venture out and do something slightly different than the other young people from their town. It may not have seemed like much, but they had made it out, made it to the city. Still they shared the same hometown roots and values. All the factors coming together made it a perfect match, and when they fell in love, they were in the prime of the lives.

Aura adored her job at the doll factory, working on an assembly line of hundreds of vinyl, painted faces. She dealt with the dolls, called Radish

Top Girls, when they were merely heads, and her task was to pull yarn through little pre-poked holes in their scalp. Each doll was supposed to be unique, so there were a lot of options for color and texture of hair. She had various types of equipment to manage it, make cuts, and even to crimp the yarn into a sort of curl. Some of the heads had a lot of holes for dolls designed to have long yarn locks that could later be collected into ponytails or pigtails using brightly colored ribbons. This was someone else's job, however; Aura didn't deal with ribbons. Other heads, that would become the baby dolls, just had a few holes in the middle for short yarn pieces to pop up like a first crop of hair.

The couple went home to be married, and the many who attended, mostly Rusty's friends and family, did scratch their heads at Rusty's choice of bride. Rusty seemed oblivious to this, but Aura noticed their sideways glances and heard the muffled comments. It had, however, felt good to spend some time with her own simple, farming parents and walk the massive acres of land she had run around on as a kid, but as soon as the event was over, Aura could not wait to get back to their cramped downtown Albany apartment where there were no people or reminders of the past to disturb the little life they had built from scratch.

She might have continued to be happy if they could have stayed put, but when they began thinking about having children, because they reached an age that they had been brought up to think was the time to think about children, Rusty thought it would be better to return home closer to their friends and families. He promised they could move back someday. Although the kids never came, other things happened. His parents got sick and then hers. He was promoted at the tannery. Time passed, and she never asked about moving because it was clear Rusty was comfortable and content just where he was.

She could have resented him for this now that he was gone, but thinking about the better days actually made her love and miss Rusty more, and when these feelings came, she did what she was taught and tucked them away as best she could.

A few weeks after Rusty's death, Aura was sitting in the same spot on the couch where she always sat knitting a scarf. She never considered moving to Rusty's recliner, even though it was more comfortable and had a better view of the television. She also never considered changing the weekly television schedule to accommodate her likes. It was a Tuesday night at 7pm, so *Wheel of Fortune* it was. She would have preferred to flip to one of those entertainment programs, but Rusty never tolerated gossip. Still in an upright position, she allowed herself to close her eyes and rest.

She quickly fell into a light dream. In the dream, she saw herself from above walking with Rusty and pushing a baby carriage. Being plagued with guilt over not being able to have children, the beginning of the dream was not so different than others she had in the past. They were walking down the main street near the apartment where they lived when they first married.

Dream Aura smiled over at Rusty who had his trademark toothpick hanging out of his mouth and his red hair shined brightly in the sun. They stopped before an intersection, and he bent down to peak into the carriage and check on their little one. It was then that the Aura from above could see the passenger in the carriage wasn't an actual baby, but one of the Radish Top Girl dolls she and her husband helped to create. The doll was absolutely precious in her striped day suit, and her long, yellow, yarn locks were immaculate if Aura didn't say so herself. Strangely, the replacement of a real baby with a doll didn't bother or disturb her in her dream or when she woke up, and even when she came fully back to reality to turn off *Jeopardy* and heat up some food for a late supper, she felt warm and good.

The next day at work she began to think of the dream as a possible sign. This was very unlike Aura, but the thoughts kept coming, no matter how she tried to suppress them as she went about her day-to-day responsibilities. Maybe she, alone, would go back to Albany now. She was still young enough; she could rent an apartment like the one she and Rusty had near the main drag and could get some kind of a job. The doll factory had long since closed, but she could type a little, and she was sure there were lots of banks in the city. She could use that money she tucked away if she absolutely needed to, and their house being near the only elementary school in town would sell as soon as it was listed.

She thought about this chance to do something no one would expect her to like she had done all those years ago when she first moved away. It would take some planning and a lot more reasoning out, of course, but who or what was there to stop her?

When she got home from work that day, there were two messages on the answering machine. She was surprised, as people had stopped calling with their condolences a week or so before, and to the best of her knowledge, all of the casserole dishes had been returned.

The messages were from her doctor's office. Her doctor had requested that she come in as soon as possible. He wanted to speak to her about a shadow on the chest x-ray he had ordered before Rusty died. Aura had forgotten about the test with all that had happened. The voice of the doctor's receptionist said she was sorry to bother her at this difficult time, but the doctor felt that, as a precaution, they shouldn't put it off. She said that he told her to tell Aura it was probably nothing and not to worry, but better to be safe than sorry.

Aura wasn't exactly worried per say, but she somehow knew right away that the shadow was not good or safe or nothing. The reason this knowing was just knowing rather than worry or fear came from an acute understanding that if something were to happen to her, it wouldn't have much of an effect. She didn't have any pets or even any plants. Her job at the bank could be done by just about anyone. Her family was gone; she had no true friends. She thought it best not to think too much about it that night and quickly settled into her evening supper and television routine, secretly hoping for another dream like the night before.

As it turned out it, Aura was right, and it was indeed something, Aura was not safe, and the doctor was very sorry when he delivered the bad news. After they heard she was sick, some of the same tannery wives who had been by in the weeks prior came again with more meals, but Aura had no desire to eat. They were again sincere in their wishes but found Aura in a much different state than before. She was talkative with them for once and even reflective. Of course, they thought it a little strange and even disturbing when Aura told them she was "fine" with the diagnosis. "I heard death is like dreaming," she said and felt warm and happy.

No one believed it when they read the obituary in the *Morning Edition* of poor "Aura Freemont Clingman, 49. Predeceased by her beloved husband by only two months." It went on to chronicle the facts of her life: career, family line, and even her dalliance in the "the city" as a dollmaker. This time there was no one to make meals for or give cards to, so people talked for about a week, maybe less, and then, with little effort, went back to life as usual.

Birthday Girl

I n a house on a great hill that looked out over the rest of the town, in a time long ago, called the mid-nineties, lived a little girl who was used to getting what she wanted. Olivia White had just turned nine years old the day before, and her birthday party – a culmination of her parents' painstaking preparations including a three tiered cake, a giant ball pit (bouncy castles were so 1991), and all the lavish gifts bestowed upon her, most notably an orange tiger kitten she named Flower Sunshine Pinky Sparkle Gumdrop White – had been, for the most part, to her utmost satisfaction. It was only one detail that had turned what should have been a perfect day sour. Luke Cole had not attended the party. Luke's mom had called and declined the invitation for her son that morning. No explanation was given. Olivia was fit to be tied and her mother, nanny, and father had to spend countless hours convincing her before she would even agree to go through with the planned event.

To be fair, Luke was a third-grade vision, and any graduated tot might be smitten. Picture: a small, tanned boy with perfectly spiked bleached blonde hair, blue eyes, straight white teeth, petite, almost mouse like, facial features – dressed in a European soccer jersey, loosely laced Adidas sneakers, a braided leather belt looped through his khaki shorts.

"I want to marry Luke," she told her friend, Penelope the next day.

"People only get married when they get pregnant, then they get divorced. Let's go cut all your Barbies' hair and color it with markers," Penelope suggested excitedly.

"My parents are still married," Olivia mused.

"Yeah, well for now, I guess. Let's go dress Flower in doll clothes and put her in a stroller or paint her claws with blue nail polish."

"I don't think Luke would want a girl who still plays with doll clothes and does childish things. Besides Flower is napping, and I don't want scratches all over my arms when I see Luke in school tomorrow."

"Okay, guess I'll go home then. Do you have any candy and cake left from the party?"

The next day Luke was not in school. And the day after that, and the day after that, and soon nearly two weeks had passed since Olivia's party.

Olivia turned herself inside out trying to cope with this separation. She didn't understand why nobody was calling *Dateline* or *Law and Order*. While not in hysterics like Olivia, after some time, the parents were talking and the children were talking. Even after the official word came from the school principal that she had received a phone call from Mrs. Cole, stating that the family, who had deep roots in the town, had moved out of state for a change of pace, the parents were still talking and the children were still talking.

The parents had their theories: a divorce, a cheating scandal, money laundering, an addiction to painkillers. The children had their own slightly more elaborate theories: Luke was buried alive in his own backyard for forgetting to take out the garbage and could now watch the grass grow over his head, Luke was stuck forever on the other side of the holes in the

Swiss cheese wall at Chucky Cheese, and other yarns along those lines.

The really funny thing about the people in a small town is that, despite whispers and speculations, they can be perfectly content never getting to the bottom of most mysteries. Maybe they are too lazy or distracted to follow through, but despite the immediate and rabid gossip, Luke Cole and his family may as well have dropped off the face of the earth for those concerned (or better put – unconcerned) and that was just fine.

Even Olivia was forced to move on in the love department with a Kurt, Mike, Sully, Dave, and finally a husband at an early age when she was pregnant with her first child. And when as little Penelope seemed to predict, Olivia found herself a divorced, twenty-something, single mother of two, finally cut off financially by her fed up parents, she began for the first time in a really long time to reflect on her long, lost first love.

Instead of bothering to ask if any friends had ever heard what became of Luke, she did what any Millennial would do, she had a few glasses of

Chardonnay courage and Googled him. But the giddiness and hope she felt moments before she touched the keys was within seconds met with disappointment and reality. A social media profile came up with a picture of a puffy, red-faced man who looked like he had soaked up too much sun, drank too many Coronas, and took too many burger runs. The man had none of the old vision's qualities, even those electric blue eyes seemed dulled and reduced to slits, but still she knew it was him. To verify, he was actually "friends" with people she was "friends" with and knew from the town. His profile even revealed that he was born there, along with a bunch of other unfavorable details about his life now.

Olivia quickly clicked the red circle in the corner of the browser. She didn't want to see or read anymore. If "friends" ever brought him up, she would refuse to listen. The Luke Cole she knew was dead, and that was that. He might as well of fallen off the face of the earth, after all – he might as well have been still looking up through the blades of grass or still peaking out from behind the cheese holes, and wasn't it better that way?

Yes, she decided in her old determined and delusional way, yes, it was.

Out-of-Towners

S ome people swore that the house was haunted, but whether that was true or not is anyone's guess now. It's hard for many us to even define what the truth is at this point: an experience, a thought, a dream, yesterday's garbage still sitting out on the curb, an unpaid phone bill. Of course, there's no denying what happened because we saw it all on tapes recorded by the family's security cameras – ironically, the ones they put in because of the supposed past hauntings.

I don't use the word tragedy lightly, but this loss has affected us all. The family was known by our small, old milling community as sensible, fair, and good. Why would something like that happen to them? Well, I'm sure you're aware of what kind of "things" they say happen to good people.

It started when the word got out to the men, who we now know take care of these types of things, that the family was going out of town. Gossip spreads like wildfire here, but how were we to know they

would find out? They were strangers, not from
around here.

On the night that it happened, almost three
years ago to the date, two of the men who take care
of these kinds of things went to the house. The man
with the gray face was much shorter and carried a
lantern that seemed to burn without a candle, almost
as if the whole thing were on fire. The larger man, a
giant really, wore a heavy, navy work suit like a
mechanic might wear and had more color to his skin,
but his features were nearly impossible to make out.
The best way to describe it would be to say that his
face looked like a smudge print on a foggy window.
He had thick, black hair that was greased back, and
his movements were slow and exaggerated like a tin
man in need of oil in his joints. This small man's
movements were the opposite; he jumped around like
an overexcited Jack Russell terrier chasing after its
owner.

When the men finally made it through the
gate and into their front yard, the larger man leaned
down and whispered something to the small man. We
couldn't hear anything at this point because the men

were still too far away from the camera on the front porch. The small man looked back at the still open gate and seemed to be riddled with fear and uncertainty. It was clear he didn't want to go any farther across the lawn, but the large man kept walking, and the small, gray man didn't want to be left behind, so he just kept hopping about after him.

When they reached the front door, the small man tried to pull on the large man's arm, but his companion didn't budge or respond to this gesture. Instead, he produced an enormous key that looked larger than the doorknob itself. It clearly wasn't the key to our neighbor's house, but although it was so big, way too big, still for some reason, it unlocked the door. "How?" the small man asked then as the lantern teetered in his shaky hand. "How you know the lives aren't to be home?"

The large man had a groggy way about him and grunted as if being woken from a nap. There was a slight pause before he flatly responded, "Out to town." And, this information should have been true.

The families, our dear neighbors, were supposed to be out of town visiting the wife's sister in

Baltimore, but the baby had had a cold the week before and still had congestion, the husband had trouble getting time off from work, and Eloise, the girl, had summer league soccer. The life of a busy family interrupted their plans, and they were very much at home.

After opening the door the men found themselves suddenly in the hall. The small man looked around anxiously; I think he might have been new to this task, maybe in training. "Sees, quiet like the church mouse," the large, possibly more experienced, man said satisfied.

"It's 3 a.m. Fred, it supposes to be quiet," the small man said. The large smudge faced man didn't look like a Fred, so I assume this was just part of their funny way of talking, funny expressions they seemed to have. They acted old fashioned or from another country or slow in speech; it was really like nothing we had heard before.

The large man picked up the wife's mother's Irish make-up bell from the side table and rang it several times but at too slow of a pace, so it produced a delayed ringing: ding...ding ding...ding...

"What's it?" he asked.

"It there be dinner bell," the small man said and shook his head vigorously agreeing with himself. The large man tried to put it in his pocket, but the small man stopped him. "That there bell not to be what we here for," he said still shaking his head. The large man, who couldn't seem to find his pocket anyway, put the bell back down on the table. Because of the weight of his movement: the way his forearm just fell from his elbow down toward the table, the bell made of the finest China smashed into pieces. The small man jumped back almost dropping his lantern.

"Uh oh, no mores dinner," the large man said unaffected.

The first bedroom they entered was Eloise's because it was the only one on the ground floor. She was moved there after the baby was born. Eloise didn't seem to mind, as long as her cat, Cheddar, was with her, which he always was. Eloise was sleeping soundly: flat on her back with her arms crossed in front of her, hands on her shoulders. Cheddar was lying at her feet.

"The little goatie there almost look like a live to be sleepin," the small, gray man said as they stood looking over Eloise, one man on each side of her bed. (Now, before you get too confused, a goatie is apparently a word the men who take care of these types of things use to mean a ghost, a spirit, some sort who is hanging around and isn't supposed to be there anymore).

"Youngs goaties supposes to be look like lives, but theys stills got to go back," the large man said, and for the first time, we could hear a little hesitation in his voice too, and if a smudge could look regretful, maybe he did. The small man poked Eloise, but she didn't move. Cheddar, on the other hand, bounded off the bed like a bolt of lightning and ran into Eloise's open closet.

The small man quickly directed the light of the lantern toward the closet. "No," the large man said. "That there kittys to be live." Then he pushed on Eloise's side in the gentlest way he seemed capable of. She still didn't stir. "Hello, I gots to take you back, little goatie," he said and began to try to lift her. Her covers were pulled tight around her, and he was having a hard time getting her free, until suddenly, Eloise woke with her eyes wide like a watchful animal. Both men stepped back from her.

She easily slipped out of the covers on her own and walked toward her door in no apparent hurry and never looking back at the men. She didn't seem to see or sense them as Cheddar had. The men did not go after her, but instead stood where they had been looking confusedly at each other.

Eloise continued into the hall and went into the family room as if looking for something. She picked up a coffee cup her father left out after his evening tea and looked inside. She licked her lips with thirst. Then she began calling, "Mama, mama, mama, mama." At her age, she wouldn't have thought to go into the kitchen, open the fridge, and pour a drink on her own. Instead, she went into the downstairs bathroom and climbed up on the toilet to have better access to the sink. She turned on the faucet and positioned herself by tilting her head to drink directly from the stream. This was something she saw

Cheddar do, often refusing to drink from a bowl like what her father considered to be a normal cat.

Next, she steadily made her way to the stairs looking behind her as she went, not for the men still in her bedroom, but for Cheddar, who usually followed her like a shadow, but with his superior, animal instincts, had abandoned her and remained deeply hidden in her closet.

She began crawling up the stairs on all fours like she did when she was younger and overtired, like she did when her bedroom was still upstairs next to her parents. She made it about halfway up the flight and laid her head down. She closed her eyes but softly still called for her mother for a time before she didn't.

After she was still and quiet, the men were instantly over and under her on the stairs. The larger man started to drag her by her feet before deciding instead to carry her over his shoulder to the bottom. "You waits here, little goatie," he said. "We soon to be back."

"That goatie sured act to be like a lives girl child," the small man said. He brought the lantern close to Eloise's face and peered at her.

"Yes, that there to be a tough, little goatie," the large man agreed. "Goaties to be like that sometimes."

They left Eloise there and went up the stairs to the collect the others. The baby and the parents were much easier to wrangle, and before the men knew it, they had the family gathered up in two sacks, both carried by the larger man, and were ready to go. They seemed more relieved than pleased with their work. Once they were out the door we could hear the large, smudge faced man humming quietly, and the smaller man asking him something barely audible, maybe: "Where there boat to be?"

The family was never returned, and we never saw the men again. I guess, the men had a job a to do, and they were given the wrong information about the live family being there by whoever is in charge of these matters. Apparently, there is no way to make up for this when a mistake has been made or they might have returned the parents and the two young children. They might still be "living" or something like living in the place they were taken. That is what we want to believe, but there is no way to know until it's our time to go there, and hopefully it will be our right time.

Some people in town view their story as a kind of lesson: like if people have vacation plans they should go, no matter what. Or if their son is supposed to go to a sleepover across the street, they should make him go even if he is crying and afraid. If they're supposed to stop for milk after work, they should even if they're running late and there's been a lot traffic. Because if they don't and just start changing plans left and right, before they know it, ghost catching men who take care of these type of things could be taking them and their family members instead.

I'm not sure if I believe this could happen again. What I believe is hard to define at this point: an experience, a thought, a dream, yesterday's garbage still sitting out on the curb, an unpaid phone bill... I guess one thing is for sure—a real nice family is gone from our town for good because they were mistaken for stubborn ghosts, they were here and then taken, and nothing has seemed the same since.

Save the Date

April is a promise that May is bound to keep.

—Hal Borland

She had everything set for the big day: the flowers, the caterer, the venue, the cake, all paid in full. The invitations had been sealed, stamped, and ready to be sent out the following Monday. It would be a small event as she wanted to be surrounded by only those who really loved and cared for them, those who truly supported their future.

As with any relationship, especially one that moved as quickly as theirs had, there were some naysayers. Her own parents and sister would not be in attendance. Of course, this betrayal hurt, but she took it all in stride; it was a sad circumstance but one that could be worked around as she had vowed not to let anyone spoil her big day. Her father would be the one she would miss most, but with his failing health even if he wanted to go against his mother's orders, it would be too much for him to travel on his own. She had promptly Googled alternatives for dealing with the pesky "giving away" part and suggestions about how to fill the space and time of the traditional father daughter dance.

There were friends who had reservations also. Most were not in all out boycott mode like her family, but they wouldn't let up on the questions. It was as though she had to justify and explain every little aspect of her decision. She had never once turned it around and questioned them on the intimate details of their personal relationships or choices, but it was fine, really fine. Everything was A-Okay, spectacular even. They had absolutely nothing to hide, she could withstand the heat, cross her t's, dot her i's, and the day would, she whole heartedly believed, go off without a hitch because nothing could ruin it, and if so it would be over her dead body, and so on.

The text message came in the middle of the night, but she didn't read it until the following morning, Sunday. Her body suddenly went numb as she leaned toward the kitchen table. She at once dropped both the phone and the "Bride-to-Be" mug she had in her other hand. The mug tumbled onto the

table and cream streaked coffee crawled toward the
stack of ivory invitations.

She came out of her shock-induced trance just
in time to snatch up the invitations and return them
to perfect order on the counter, and oh, what a relief
that was. She repeated her mantra, safe and sound,
and let out a breath. She had adverted disaster, and
this wasn't the first time. She felt almost silly. It was
simply not like her to overreact in that manner. The
trivial little message didn't even matter; he didn't
mean it; he was probably drunk. It was her day after
all, and she would just have to get creative and find a
clever and tactful way, a loving way, to make him
understand that no one was going to take this away
from her.

Replacement Witch

S he knew when she saw the blood in the snow during the terrible winter of 1978 that she had both lost and gained her most beautiful rivals. The jealousy that defined her would only become more evil because now she envied a motherless little baby as only the most crooked could. And she abhorred the affection that was even stronger than the ardent passion father felt for mother, the unconditional love a parent has for their own child. Still she was able to bed and wed the man within months of my mother's passing. I grew up wondering whether it was fear or simple necessity as he traveled so much for his work, and if he were to be honest with himself, to suit his nature, but I knew it was not real love despite Hazel's once starlet looks. I have always been a great reader and prone to fantasies, but in no world, fairy or otherwise, could that kind of love be reconciled.

From infanthood, I was praised for my beauty and temperament. At first Hazel tried to embrace it for her own gain, even entering me in the type of children's showcases she herself had placed so highly in, but there was one striking problem. Yes, striking is the word most used to describe my resemblance to my mother, the most worthy beauty queen to have never entered the race. Yet, just as no outside admiration could absolve my guilt over causing my mother's death, there were no comparisons that went unnoted by Hazel as she sank deeper into the evil stepmother archetype. The woman was illustration ready; she became that good at looking so good while being so bad.

As I grew older, the problem of my resemblance to mother was overshadowed by the simple premise of the passage of time. I was growing older into mature womanhood, and Hazel was growing older past her prime. As a child, she had either ignored me or propped me up as an alternate version of my mother's daughter, one that was more in her reflection. She didn't nurture or add, but she didn't really harm or take. I was there as a reflection or not there at all in her eyes. But, if I could summarize her treatment of me once I became about thirteen years old, I would say, she took and took and took until there was so little left that even in my own eyes, I was either not there or a mere reflection. She took with her words, she took with her attack on my memories, she took by driving my father farther away from her and thus by situation, me.

As for my father, he could have tried harder, but he did try. He tried to help with therapy and once offered to work from home to keep watch over me and what Hazel described as my tendencies to be self-destructive. She had so successfully painted me as fragile. In his eyes, I was as fragile as the undisturbed bird skeleton we found in his office closet when I was a child. Something to be admired, but never touched, never tampered with. If he wasn't there, it eliminated the possibility of him crushing me with one misdirected step. Others who loved or would have loved me felt similarly. No one wanted to be responsible. Having had my own burden of guilt to carry, I could not blame them for keeping a distance.

During the summer of 1993, I somehow managed to find a boyfriend, or I guess it was the boy who found me, and he wanted to be with me, so in essence he was probably pretty messed up himself.

On the early August night that my story changed, it was particularly hot and without the characteristic sea breeze that can fend off a New England meltdown. Hazel and I had fought, and by fought I mean Hazel had stuck to her habit of taking the normal ingredients of self-loathing, worthlessness, and desperation out of her magic bag and flung them at me to see which would stick. Despite her most deviant efforts, this night, I decided I was going to a party with my boy in a neck of the woods by the edge of town that they call Hack's point. I had never wanted to go to a party before, so Hazel had no reason to tell me I wasn't allowed to go to parties, and my assertiveness caught her so off guard that it sent her fuming and scrambling in search of other tricks.

Alone, I made a decision that would change everything. I'm not sure what possessed me exactly, perhaps it was nothing more than the simple fact I did not own a mirror, but while Hazel was stewing in the steamy downstairs pantry, I went into her bedroom. This had been the bedroom that my mother and father once shared, but for as long as I could remember it was Hazel's room and off limits to all but the lady herself.

My father slept in the den when he was home, and his clothes and belongings were mostly in the storage room adjacent to the garage. Hazel kept the door to her room closed, whether she was in there or not, so my main associations were the visceral and sensory variety. Through the slit under the door I had viewed strange colors, dark, light, felt coldness, and sometimes heard muffled sounds. I smelled the musty stench of old clothes and of burning herbs. This was how I knew her room, and nothing about it ever called come hither. Every part of my body and soul went into warning mode when I passed until this night.

Although I had never been in the room, I knew there was a mirror because I had heard father's complaints about her spending so much time in front of it. She was obsessed with primping and prepping, and when I came inside I could see the dressing room type lights and arrangements of little tokens around the mirror that made it the centerpiece. Surely every item had been carefully considered to set the mood and make her look her best, always the best. While I tried to take in specifics: what was in these bottles, what did the markings on that book mean, what was it making those strange sounds, I was drawn only to the mirror, compelled to focus on it and only it, beyond my purpose for being there. I saw myself, and for the first time my beauty struck me like it had struck others. It stung like being slapped, yet ached like being punched. The mirror called my mother's name, and before I knew it I saw only red and tasted blood.

I must have sat down before the mirror because of the location of my injuries. It was the weight I felt, sure, but also the way the glass pieces rained down on me. It was not so much specific pain, but an unfamiliar awareness of feeling in general. I waited to hear my own name, for a word of correction or explanation, but the shattered mirror had nothing else to say.

Soon I found myself back in the hallway and looking for Hazel for the first time in my life. I wanted to show her what her mirror did to me. She immediately tried to distance herself with excuses and

divert all blame as she circled around me not
comprehending for once I was not blaming her.
Despite the words coming out of her mouth, her look
was one of satisfaction or hope or both.

They say the mirror unhinged from the vanity
because its rusty fixtures finally gave way. They called
it a freak accident, nothing anyone could have
predicted since the piece was hundreds of years old.
Who could know exactly when this would happen or
that the four would go at the same time? Yes, I
thought, who could and who would.

Now months later on the outside not much
has changed, and only the stains and scars remain to
tell the story, but the jagged blessings etched across
my face may be the real heroes. They now serve as
permanent protection from my beauty and fear of
losing it. They prevent others from worrying about
the fragility of my perfection any longer and have
opened the door to a world of fractured endings.

Whether I go on to find romantic love or
have children of my own, I'm now free to seek out all
the motherless little creatures of the world that I've
always been drawn to and say—I'm your mother,

you're never alone. I don't have to fulfill any other destiny but the one my mother was denied. I wonder if stepmother had seen this all of this in her cards, or if Hazel was just as pleasantly surprised to find the replacement witch is as good as dead.

Formal Introductions

Peter, Peter, pumpkin eater,
Had a wife, and couldn't keep her;
He put her in a pumpkin shell,
And there he kept her very well.

S cene One: également appelé—The One and Only
Scene:

No one, not one, knew Mr. Peters even had a
wife, especially not his bubbly blonde, aspiring
starlet/part-time burlesque dancer/secretary/three
months pregnant girlfriend, Mandy (stage name Cecily
Parsley), although it didn't take long for the news to
spread in their tight-knit community.

Turns out the wife's name was Margaret, and
that was the only back-story provided. She arrived on
a Monday by taxi, according to at least two
eyewitnesses, and strode down Main Street toward
Mr. Peters' office with all the airs of a successful
lawyer's spouse and a slight limp. She carried no
luggage aside from a purse sized and shaped like a
bowling bag.

Mr. Peters was alone in his office when the temp let Margaret in on the woman's word, so no one heard that initial conversation between them. It was the temp's first day filling in for Mandy, who was on an audition, so she wouldn't have known then that the wife's visit was out of the ordinary.

After that day, conversations between the direct parties involved were just as secretive. No details were provided by Mr. Peters, Margaret, or Mandy, and out of respect or confusion, no one asked. What kind of damage control Mr. Peters had to do with Mandy is a mystery, but she never brought up the situation in any capacity to any person, no one, not even one. And whenever Margaret met someone new, even Mr. Peters' closest friends, who most wives would already know, she would politely put out her hand and say something like, "Oh, how silly is this? I know all about you, and I'm sure my husband has told you all about me, but I don't think we've formally met."

Margaret seemed to thrive in her role and went from being non-existent in the town to being seemingly everywhere, especially at Mr. Peters' side.

Despite being friendly with others, she relentlessly badgered Mr. Peters. Usually an assertive kind of guy, he went along without protest. The hen-pecked man appeared to have aged 10 years within the first week.

The temp at his practice soon replaced Mandy permanently. She was also let go from the gentlemen's club as her pregnancy was starting to show. Unlike social Margaret, Mandy kept pretty much out of sight, but when people did see her, their reports weren't good.

Then about a month after his wife's arrival, Mr. Peters came into the office looking refreshed. The former temp, now permanent, asked where Margaret was as she had even taken to following him into work. He told her that she had to go out of town for a few days, and that he himself would be taking off the rest of the day to tend to some personal business. He asked the permanent, although he said he hated to with her being so new, "Would you please be a dear, my dear, and mind the old fort?"

About ten minutes after Mr. Peters left, a sort of youngish, sort of prettyish woman, who the permanent had never seen before, came stumbling through the door. Her makeup was smeared, her open jacket torn, and her crop top revealed what looked like a small beer belly. She put out her hand, introduced herself with strange formality as Miss Cecily Parsley, fiancé to Mr. Peters, and asked if he was in. The permanent feeling compelled to introduce herself as the former temp went on to say that Mr. Peters had left and tentatively, without trying to be rude, asked the strange visitor, who she suspected to be Mandy, although never crossing paths with her predecessor, whether she needed some other help or wanted to clean up in the restroom. Cecily/Mandy looked through her and didn't answer before disappearing out the door from which she came – without a trace, as they say.

And so it was later said, the arrival of one, led to the departure of three as no one around our town ever saw Mandy or Mr. Peters or Margaret again, thus we could only speculate with a wink or a sign on a next scene/ending for any or all of the sad, little cast of characters.

Eeper Weeper, chimney sweeper,
Had a wife but couldn't keep her.
Had another, didn't love her,
Up the chimney he did shove her.

Ω